ZUGGY

THE RESCUE PUG

🐾 SIX TALES 🐾

JEAN
MARIE
ALFIERI

Zuggy the Rescue Pug – Six Tales
Written by Jean Marie Alfieri
Illustrations by Alexandra Ruiz
Graphic Design and Layout by Christine Sterling-Bortner

Copyright 2020 All rights reserved.
Second Edition – August 2020
Originally published by Newman Springs Publishing 2018

ISBN: 978-1-7343086-0-0

Dedication

To dog lovers and those blessed with the good fortune of ever being loved by a pug! Special thanks to my husband and son, for all your support and encouragement. ~JMA

To my friends and family who have been ever so supportive. And to all the fur-parents who love their fur-kids unconditionally. ~AR

SIX TALES

Zuggy the Rescue Pug
Snow Day

Flakes started to fall.
And continued all night.
A swirling snow globe.
A soft blanket of white.

The kids were joyous.
School was closed for the day!
They got bundled up
To go out and play.

They built a snowman
But didn't have a hat,
So on top of his head,
A sombrero sat.

Zuggy watched them work.
They were having great fun.
Stick arms and a scarf,
The snow hombre was done.

Inside for cocoa,
They filled up their mugs.
"Let's go out with Zuggy!"
"Bark-Bark," said the pug.

Pearl covered his ears
And zipped up his sweater.
He'd be nice and warm
In the icy cold weather

Roy opened the door.
Zuggy bounded ahead.
He tried to run fast
But slipped and slid instead.

Skidding on his butt
And zooming toward the stair.
Roy tried to snag him
But missed by a hair!

Flying past the step,
Zuggy gave a loud "Ruff!"
He soared through the air
Landing in a great "PUFF!"

Then all was silent.
Not a sound from the snow.
Pearl wondered out loud,
"Where'd that silly pug go?"

The snowman trembled.
He'd been hit pretty hard.
Then a great earthquake
Shuddered through the whole yard.

The kids turned to see
Zuggy pop through the snow.
He felt a 'Ker-plunk' -
"Where'd everyone go?!"

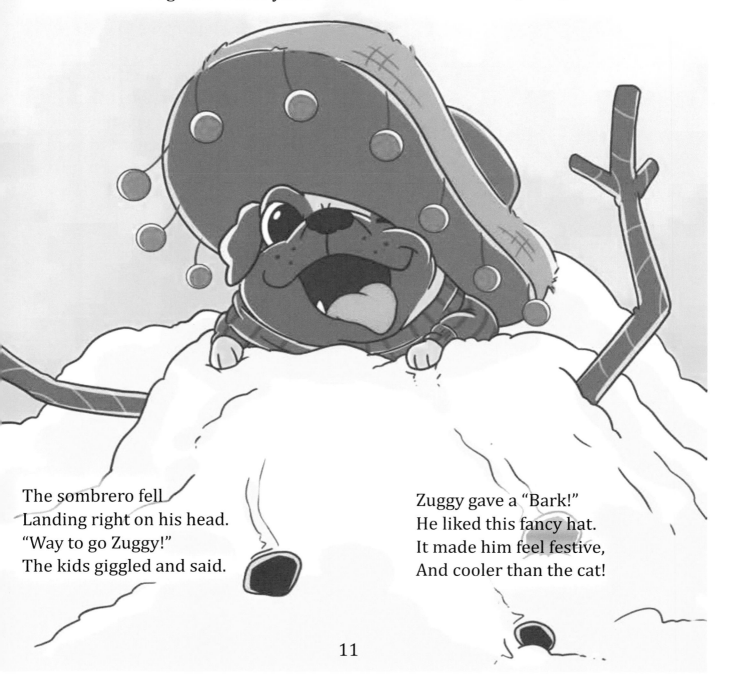

The sombrero fell
Landing right on his head.
"Way to go Zuggy!"
The kids giggled and said.

Zuggy gave a "Bark!"
He liked this fancy hat.
It made him feel festive,
And cooler than the cat!

Zuggy the Rescue Pug
Baker's Dozen

Zuggy likes weekends,
And Sundays are the best!
His people go to church.
He stays home to rest.

Then they come home with
A box of luscious treats.
Super sweet goodness.
That smell is hard to beat!

Frosted with sprinkles,
White powdered with jelly,
Long ones and twisted ones.
A growl from his belly!

Set on the counter,
Dad opens the box.
Zuggy creeps in low.
He's sneaky like a fox!

His mouth watering,
Zuggy gives a loud howl.
Mom says, "Stop drooling!"
As she swipes with her towel.

13

Dad grabs a donut
Then fills up his mug.
He turns around and trips
On that tricky little pug!

Dad watches it fall
And roll across the floor.
Zuggy chases it
As it speeds toward the door.

Zuggy takes a leap
To pounce that Boston Cream.
And right in his face
Squirts a thick custard stream!

It covers his muzzle.
He happily licks.
About to chow down -
But Mom gets there right quick.

She nabs the donut
Out from under his paw.
Mom made sure that it was
The last of it he saw.

Zuggy paced around,
Not willing to give up.
Someone had to give in.
He was their favorite pup!

Mom went to the box.
Zuggy's bulging eyes grew.
"Here you go, Zuggy.
Made special for you!"

He tasted tart apples
And a hint of sweet butter.
He gulped it right down
And looked up for another.

Zuggy loved the treat
And could have eaten four,
But he was happy
When Mom gave him one more!

Zuggy the Rescue Pug
The Walk

Zuggy loves walking
When the weather is nice.
Fresh air and flowers
Are like sugar and spice.

Mom tugs on his leash.
It's time they move along.
Zuggy catches a scent.
It's sassy, sweet and strong.

Zuggy sniffs the breeze,
Nose high up in the air.
He turns and sees her.
Zuggy can't help but stare.

Gabby is stunning.
A dog, but not like him.
Her coat sleek and grey.
Her body long and slim.

Zuggy jumps the curb
And starts to cross the street.
"This canine super model,
I simply have to meet!"

He runs out of leash
And is suddenly stopped.
Glancing back at Mom,
He barks, fusses and hops.

"We don't even know them,"
Zuggy hears Mom say.
"Exactly!" he barks back,
"Why should we delay?"

He barks all the more.
Mom orders him to "Stay."
Zuggy leans and pulls
As Gabby walks away.

It happened so fast.
Zuggy got himself free.
Not seeing the cars,
Zuggy ran down the street.

Gabby sprang from the curb.
She barked out to him.
Could he make it to her?
His chances looked slim.

With great greyhound speed
She was there in a flash.
Zuggy was amazed
At how fast she could dash!

He heard a car honk
And the loud screech of brakes.
Might this be a nightmare
From which he would wake?

17

It swerved to a halt
Just inches from them.
Zuggy opened his eyes
And saw his new friend.

A strong hand reached down,
And picked Zuggy up.
Shivering and panting -
The poor frightened pup.

18

Gabby had saved him.
He gave her a hug.
She risked her own life
For a stout little pug!

Zuggy is thankful
He met Gabby that day.
They love being friends,
And together they play.

Zuggy the Rescue Pug
Friend or Foe

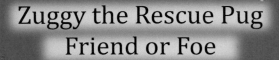

The low overnight
Was 80 degrees.
Summer in the desert.
There's barely a breeze.

Mom is up early.
The best time to walk.
Dad likes to join her.
They sip coffee and talk.

They hike up the road,
Alongside a mountain.
Then stop in their tracks.
Something moves by the fountain.

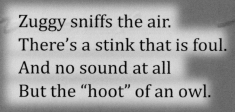

Zuggy sniffs the air.
There's a stink that is foul.
And no sound at all
But the "hoot" of an owl.

Mom whispers to Dad.
She keeps her voice low.
"What's that in the shadows?
A friend or a foe?"

Is it the scared squirrel
Who scampers away
When Zuggy gives chase?
Just trying to play.

Or the mean kitty cat
Who uses her tail
To invite him to pounce,
Then fights with her nails?

A small figure steps out
As if to say "Hi."
He's about Zuggy's size.
A sweet little guy.

21

Zuggy steps forward,
"I'm ready to play!"
Dad tightens his leash
And tells him to "Stay."

A grunt from behind.
A large figure appears.
Momma Javelina
And she shows no fear.

With tusks big and pointy,
And a coat that is rough.
Though pigs can be cute,
This one's rather gruff.

She looks right at Zuggy
And lowers her head.
Dad has to move fast.
Mom's frozen with dread.

Zuggy is hoisted
And tucked under arm.
They back away slowly
To avoid any harm.

22

The pigs grunt and snort.
They then move along.
Soon Zuggy's set down
Next to his front lawn.

"What an adventure!"
A great start to the day.
Now safe back at home
Zuggy likes it that way.

Zuggy the Rescue Pug
Stormy Weather

It rumbled in the morning
And through the afternoon.
Zuggy dashed around and barked.
Not knowing what to do.

He heard the dishes rattle
With each crack of thunder.
How would anyone survive?
He was left to wonder.

He hid under the table,
On the shaggy blue rug.
Then curled up in his blanket
Where he often felt snug.

Another clap of thunder,
Then a bolt of lightning.
Rain drummed against the windows.
It was very frightening.

He threw his head back and howled.
From room to room he paced.
Zuggy felt nervous and stressed.
Dad saw it on his face.

His howl became a whimper
As Zuggy braved the storm.
He never liked bad weather,
Not since he was born.

His little brother, Chico,
Brought the fuzzy lion.
He dropped the toy at his paws
So Zuggy might stop cryin'.

Dad sits down and calls to them.
The pups lay in his lap.
A place they feel safe and warm.
They close their eyes to nap.

Stars are shining when they wake.
The storm has finally passed.
Dad hustles them outside.
A potty break at last!

Zuggy the Rescue Pug
Unlucky Step

Too chilly outside.
Zuggy doesn't like snow.
He laid on the rug.
Not a chance he would go.

Mom bundled him up.
Wind whipped through the door.
He plopped his butt down.
His paws clung to the floor.

Mom tapped his bottom.
He reluctantly trudged.
Not happy with this.
He'd hold on to this grudge!

He pulled like a horse
And gave his leash a tug.
"Whose walk is this, Mom?!"
Barked Zuggy the Pug.

Not seeing the danger,
Off the sidewalk he flew.
Felt something go SQUISH
Had he stepped in dog poo?!

Just slightly frozen,
It glommed on to his paw.
He kicked and he shook.
Mom was shocked when she saw!

She started to laugh.
Zuggy wiggled and danced.
That poo stuck like glue
So he started to prance.

In a small snow mound,
He tried to wipe it away.
If caught doing this,
What would anyone say?

He was embarrassed.
All his dog friends would stare!
A stinky poo-paw.
This was such a nightmare!

Mom tried to help him.
But he wouldn't calm down.
On only three paws
He kept hopping around!

He thrust out his leg
In a great round-house kick.
He checked his back paw.
It continued to stick.

He tried it again.
Maybe this time it'd work.
Forward then backward,
He wriggled and jerked.

One last mighty kick.
His persistence was key.
The poo went sailing.
And Zuggy was free!

ABOUT THE POET AND HER PUG

Jean knew when her eyes locked with those of a smooshy-faced little dog, who sat inside a kennel at her local Humane Society, that it was love at first sight.

He captured her heart and she captured some of their many adventures in sweet short story poems starring her often mischievous and always adorable rescue pug named Zuggy.

Jean enjoys visiting school and community events, sharing these light-hearted and beautifully illustrated books. See their fun photo gallery at: www.ZuggythePug.com

Want more Zuggy?

***Zuggy the Rescue Pug –
Adoption Day***

Check out these two Zuggy
books available on Amazon!
Get your copy (Paperback or
Kindle) today!

***Zuggy the Rescue Pug –
Bellyache Blues***

And remember to visit us at ZuggyThePug.com!

Made in United States
Troutdale, OR
07/04/2024